The *Evening* King

by
David LaRochelle

illustrated by
Catherine Stock

ATHENEUM · 1993 · NEW YORK

Maxwell Macmillan Canada
Toronto

Maxwell Macmillan International
New York Oxford Singapore Sydney

Atheneum
Macmillan Publishing Company
866 Third Avenue
New York, NY 10022

Maxwell Macmillan Canada, Inc.
1200 Eglinton Avenue East
Suite 200
Don Mills, Ontario M3C 3N1

Macmillan Publishing Company is part of the Maxwell Communication Group of Companies.

First edition

Printed in Hong Kong by South China Printing Company (1988) Ltd.

10   9   8   7   6   5   4   3   2   1

The text of this book is set in Sabon.

The illustrations are rendered in watercolor.

LIBRARY OF CONGRESS CATALOGING-IN-PUBLICATION DATA
LaRochelle, David.
        The evening king/David LaRochelle.
            p.   cm.
        Summary: A young boy pretends to be a sea captain,
explorer, giant, magician, monster, and king.
            ISBN 0-689-31640-2
        [1. Imagination—Fiction.]   I. Title.
        PZ7.L3234Ev   1993
        [E]—dc20   91–1970

To Greg Clark
—D. L.

Sometimes when the clouds grow thick,
the wind roars through the cottonwood trees,
and the raindrops fall small and hard . . .

I stand on our picnic table and shout into the storm,
"Pirates on the starboard side, mates!
Draw your swords and be brave."
I am the sea captain, daring and tall,
whose courage is envied by all in my crew.

"You're going to get wet," calls the neighbor lady
as she hurries to take in her wash.

Sometimes when the air is still and hot
and the leaves hang exhausted from the trees . . .

I climb through a maple jungle
and wrestle the dangling python waiting for me.
I am the explorer of lost worlds.
Danger is my trade.

"Don't wear yourself out," warns my mother.
"You'll get heatstroke."

Sometimes in the tall yellow grass
by the side of our house
where the crickets and ants escape from the sun . . .

I stomp through a forest of towering trees
while the people run for cover.
My voice is a thundering wave when I shout,
"I am the giant of the valley, here to reclaim my land!"
At the last moment, I decide to spare their village
and make friends.

"Haven't you finished the weeding?" asks my dad.

Sometimes when our house hums and clatters
with the sound of cleaning . . .

the crayons in my room chase each other around my notebook,
making numbers and shapes that I balance and toss.
Even the pencils cannot remain still
when I snap my fingers.
I am the keeper of magic, making rivers of color
flow out of my hands.

"Those stubs are too short to use," says my sister
as she waves a dust rag.
"Throw them away."

Sometimes when the boredom of Sundays is too much
to bear . . .

I summon up monsters of music and noise,
and together we dance on the chairs
and the walls and the bed.
With my whole body I scream, "I am the loudest creature alive!
No one can stop me and no one will try!"

"Turn down that radio," my family yells back.

In the evening, when everyone else is asleep
or downstairs . . .

I look out my window down to the pond
where the moon is two silver coins.

Then I am the Evening King,
who stands quiet and alone,
and in peace, I count my treasure.